Affectionately dedicated
to my mother, Eloise Wilkin,
whose illustrations
were the inspiration
for this book.

D.W.S.

Library of Congress Cataloging-in-Publication Data

Springett, Deborah Wilkin
  Eloise Wilkin's book of poems.

  "A Golden book."
  Summary: A dozen poems about familiar early
childhood experiences.
  1. Children's poetry, American. [1. American poetry]
I. Wilkin, Eloise, ill. II. Title.
PS3545.I367E57   1988   811'.54   86-22480
ISBN: 0-307-15838-1
ISBN: 0-307-65838-4 (lib. bdg.)

Eloise Wilkin's
BOOK of POEMS

Poems by **Deborah Wilkin Springett**
Paintings by **Eloise Wilkin**

A GOLDEN BOOK • NEW YORK

Western Publishing Company, Inc., Racine, Wisconsin 53404

Sitting by the Shore

Tumbling over rocks and sand,
Whitecaps leap upon the land,
Crashing with a mighty roar.
Sea gulls hover near the shore.

Rocky pools formed by the tide
Make a place for crabs to hide.
Nestled in the sand I find
Shells the waves have left behind.

Flocks of sanderlings explore
Back and forth along the shore.
Castles that I build stand tall,
Washed by waves they break and fall.

Driftwood I throw out to sea
Waves will push right back to me.
Dreams are made and spirits soar
When I sit here by the shore.

A Rainy Day

Rain falls gently all around,
Puddles form then on the ground.

Wet leaves rustle in the breeze,
Small birds huddle in the trees.

Rainbows arch across the sky,
Long fat worms on dirt paths lie.

Storm clouds slowly drift away,
Fresh scents linger through the day.

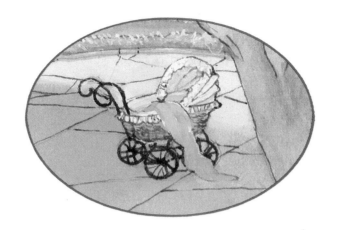

The Tea Party

I sit beneath the apple tree
And pour my dolls some cambric tea.
I like to add a lump or two
Of sugar to this special brew.

My dolls and I can hardly wait
To taste the tea cake on each plate.
I always have enough for me
When my three dollies come to tea.

The Pouting Chair

I didn't mean to tease the cat
Or lose my brother's baseball bat.
I got a scolding after that.
        I'm sitting in my pouting chair.
        I'd pout all day, but who would care?

I didn't mean to mess the den
Or break my sister's fountain pen.
I got a spanking once again.
        I'm sitting in my pouting chair.
        I'd pout all day, but who would care?

To pout all day is not much fun,
So for today my pouting's done.
I'll say, "I'm sorry, everyone."
        Now if I promise to take care
        May I please leave my pouting chair?

A Pet's Duet

I practice every day at three.
My dog named Bo does, too, you see.
Bo likes to howl along with me,
Although his howling is off-key.

However, he does very well
Each time I play "The First Noel."
(His favorite song, if he could tell,
Is called "The Farmer in the Dell.")

Sometimes my parents get upset.
I tell them why they shouldn't fret:
Not every child can boast a pet
Who likes to howl in a duet.

A Child Is Sick

"My darling, hush,
    Your mother's here.
Now let me wipe
    Away each tear.

"Do you feel sick?
    Please try to tell.
This medicine
    Can make you well."

With tender hands
    She smooths his brow.
Her little boy
    Feels better now.

Soft moonlight shines
    Down from the sky
As Mother sings
    A lullaby.

She asks the Lord
    Her child to keep
And gently rocks
    Her son to sleep.

English Schoolgirls

Away to see the London Zoo
March English schoolgirls, two by two,

In uniforms of blue and red,
A yellow boater on each head.

Their leader is Miss Hannah Poole,
Headmistress of Saint Hilda's School.

She warns the girls that they must mind
To keep in step, not lag behind.

No books to read, no sums to do,
They're off to see the London Zoo.

The Magic of a Winter Day

The magic of a winter day—
    Last night there was a freeze.
The sky is overcast and gray,
    A frost is on the trees.

The magic of a soft snowflake—
    It floats down to the ground,
And others floating in its wake
    Spread beauty all around.

The magic of a brisk sleigh ride—
    As down the hill I go,
My sled begins to slide and glide,
    And I land in the snow!

The magic of a tall snowman
    We build on our front lawn—
We stack him up as best we can
    And hope he lasts till dawn.

The magic of a winter night—
    All snuggled in my bed,
My dreams are filled, to my delight,
    With magic days ahead.

Eloise Wilkin

The Meadow

In meadowlands where creatures stay,
A child sits in quiet play.

She picks the flowers left by rain
And slowly weaves a daisy chain.

It's fun to watch the clouds drift by
And make their patterns in the sky.

A furry rabbit sits and feeds,
Two butterflies flit through the weeds.

Loud, raucous crows are on the wing,
A meadowlark begins to sing.

These are her playmates, large and small,
God's precious creatures, one and all.

My Sad Glad Face

Two days ago my face was sad.
    My parents took a trip that day,
    That's why my grandma came to stay.
    I cried as their car drove away.

Next day my face was almost glad.
    My grandma planned some things to do.
    We baked a cake and cookies, too,
    And visited the county zoo.

Today my face is really glad.
    My mom and dad call every day,
    And even though they're far away,
    I'm glad my grandma came to stay.

BY MARK GRANDMA

At Sunset

From Grandma's house we're homeward bound
As dusk begins its evening round.

The snow that's fallen on our street
Makes crunching sounds beneath our feet.

The sky glows red at close of day—
We marvel at the sun's display.

The sun sinks downward in the west
As horse and sleigh come home to rest,

And little footsteps in the snow
Trail homeward in the afterglow.

Moonlight Through the Window

The night's coming soon,
I watch for the moon,
Which floats through the sky like a giant balloon.

The shadows I see,
From each maple tree,
Reach out to the window and almost touch me.

I watch the moon glide
Over fields far and wide—
Its silvery glow lights the whole countryside.

The moon shines all night,
A beacon of light—
Before morning comes it will fade out of sight.